DONALD DUCK

BIG LITTLE BOOK

CLASSIC

Big Little Book® Classics are all-time favorites from the past, representing the best of over six hundred titles. The publishers are proud to bring back these time-proven Classics in response to the overwhelming reader request.

SEE DONALD DANCE
THE HULA

Flip the pages rapidly and watch the pictures in upper right-hand corner as the characters seem to come alive!

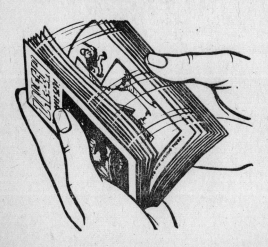

WALT DISNEY

Presents

DONALD DUCK

in

VOLCANO VALLEY

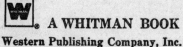 A WHITMAN BOOK

Western Publishing Company, Inc.

Racine, Wisconsin

CONTENTS

Window-Shopping

CHAPTER 1

A BIG BARGAIN

Donald Duck and his three nephews stopped in front of the display window of a hobby shop one day. The article that had attracted their attention was a model airplane with a fifteen-dollar price tag on it.

"Unca Donald—" began Huey.

"Will you buy us—" added Dewey.

"A model plane, huh?" finished Louie.

"Not at that price," Donald answered. "I can get one from the government surplus people for much less. The army had lots of them during the war." He finally drew his nephews away from the window and started toward home. The boys pouted.

"I'll write for one right now," Donald promised his nephews as

Donald Explains

he stepped into the house.

"Aw, that'll take forever," the boys grumbled to each other.

Donald found an official price listing for model planes.

"Here's a three-foot model of an experimental bomber for only two dollars and fifty cents. I'll order that," he said. He filled out the order blank, enclosed a check, and sent the boys to mail the letter.

The boys waited impatiently for a reply. Weeks later, when they had almost forgotten about it, they

Ordering the Model Plane

found a letter in the mailbox that sent them racing into the house.

"Unca Donald, here's a letter for you—" said Dewey.

"From the—" said Louie.

"Government Surplus Depot," finished Huey.

They waited excitedly while Donald opened the letter.

"It must be to tell me that they've shipped the model plane I ordered," Donald said. The boys watched their uncle's face as he read the letter.

Good News

"Yeah! They sent it! But we have to go across town to pick it up," Donald told them. Huey, Louie, and Dewey were overjoyed. They jumped up and down and turned handsprings.

"Let's go!" shouted Louie.

They ran as fast as they could to the garage and were ready to go before Donald could pick up his hat.

The letter had directed him to go to the airplane landing field. Donald went to the office and gave

Overjoyed Nephews

the letter to the man sitting at the desk.

"I'm here to get this plane and take it home with me," Donald said.

"Take it home? Are you trying to kid me?" the man asked in astonishment.

"No. I'm not kidding. It's for my nephews here to play with. Where is it?" Donald asked. The man shrugged. Then he opened a door and beckoned to them.

"Your nephews must be tougher than they look. Follow me," he

Presenting the Letter

said. Donald and his nephews followed the man down a long hall and through a doorway. They found themselves outside on a runway of the landing field. Straight ahead was a huge airplane. The man from the office pointed to it.

"Number B-one-nine-seven-Z-NG. That's it, mister!" he said.

"A giant bomber! But I only ordered a *model* three feet long— for two dollars and fifty cents!" Donald protested.

"If there's been a mistake, it's

"That's It, Mister!"

your hard luck. You must take what is sent you—and there'll be no refunds on your money," the man said, shrugging his shoulders.

Donald was indignant, but the man was no longer interested. He walked away without another word.

"Of all the crazy deals," Donald fumed. "Here I pay two-fifty for a tiny model plane, and they send me a four-engine bomber."

Donald was so busy raving that he failed to notice a dark stranger,

An Indignant Donald

wearing a large sombrero and a striped serape, standing nearby. There was a suitcase at his side. He started toward Donald with his hand outstretched.

"Eef you no like eet, *señor*, I weel geef you three dollars for eet," he said with a big smile.

Donald cheered up and began to consider the offer. His nephews watched him in astonishment.

"Three dollars. That makes me a nice profit. I'll—" Donald said and started to walk toward the

The Stranger Approaches

stranger. Huey, Louie, and Dewey exchanged glances. Knowing they would have to do something in a hurry if they were to stop him, the three boys tackled their uncle and threw him to the ground.

"Don't be a sap, Unca Donald!" said Huey.

"Those bombers cost millions," said Louie.

"The junkman'll give you at least a hundred dollars for it," Dewey whispered into his ear.

Donald gave the matter further

Convincing Uncle Donald

thought as he struggled to his feet. He decided the boys were right. Brushing himself off, he approached the would-be buyer.

"I consider your offer too low, mister. You'll have to raise your bid—much, much higher," Donald said.

The stranger bit his lip, lowered his head, and paced back and forth in a worried manner.

"I come from Volcanovia, *señor!*" the stranger began. "And I would buy thees plane for

Worried Volcanovian

my contree, but we are not a reech
contree." He stopped and held out
both arms in a gesture of appeal.

"Weeth tears een my eyes I make
you grand offer—three hundred
thousand Volcanovian pezozies," he
said. Then he bowed.

Donald's expression changed to
delight. His head whirled at the
thought of sudden riches. He shook
hands with the stranger.

"Well, now, that's better. I'll take
your offer, Mr. What's-Your-
Name," Donald said.

"I'll Take Your Offer."

The man made a sweeping bow, and again his face broke into a broad smile. "Major Pablo Mañana! Volcanovia's most honored son, *señor!*" he introduced himself.

Donald introduced himself and his three nephews. Major Mañana made another low bow. Then he opened the suitcase. Donald's eyes almost popped out when he saw the contents—paper money.

"Here, *señor*, ees your three hundred thousand pezozies. Would you like a ride in the plane before

A Money-Filled Suitcase

I fly eet to my contree?" he asked.

Donald was speechless with his sudden wealth, but the boys were eager to go.

"Gee, Unca Donald, we *do* want a ride!" said Huey.

"Please, Unca Donald," coaxed Louie.

"Let's go up!" pleaded Dewey. Major Mañana turned his genial smile on the boys.

"Ha! Pablo feex! Your uncle buy some gas for the tanks, I take you for a good ride," he promised.

Eager to Go

All four turned eager eyes toward Donald. Donald looked up at the huge plane with its four motors, and then at the stack of money.

"Why not? I'm a rich man. Attendant! Gas this bus! Fill her up," he said with a majestic wave of his hand.

The attendant signaled to someone in the hangar, and a big tank truck drove up alongside the bomber. It seemed to take forever to fill the tank. Then it took more time for the attendant to figure out

"Fill Her Up!"

the bill. He finally looked up.

"She took four thousand gallons, bud. That'll be twelve hundred dollars. Pay me," he said.

Donald almost fainted at the size of the bill.

"Twelve hundred dollars!" he gasped. He looked longingly at his big pile of paper money. "That's a lot of hay," Donald said. "But here, take it out of this stack." The attendant was amazed at the amount of money until he got a closer look at it. Then he shook his

Twelve-Hundred-Dollar Bill

head and snorted in disgust.

"Volcanovian pezozies! Don't hand me that stuff!" he shouted at Donald.

"What?" Donald cried.

"A hayrack full of that lettuce wouldn't make twelve hundred dollars. What you have there is worth about three dollars," the attendant explained.

At first Donald refused to believe his ears, but he could tell by the expression on the attendant's face that he was not trying to be funny.

Worthless Money

Donald clapped his hand to his head and jumped up and down in rage.

"I've sold that plane for three dollars! Oh, have I been taken!" Donald moaned.

"And you'll be taken to jail if you don't pay this twelve hundred dollars! Start digging, bud!"

"I—I haven't that much money, but—" Donald stammered and looked around in panic.

"But what?"

"I have a car over there! It's—

"I've Been Taken!"

well, it's all I've got," Donald said.
Donald hopped in and started the
car while the attendant looked it
over.

"Hmm!" said the attendant.
"1920 Mixwell engine, 1922 Dudge
body, 1923 Paclac axles, wheels in
bad shape. But it runs. Okay, I'll
take the car and call it square."

Looking Her Over

CHAPTER 2

UP IN THE AIR

Sadder, but wiser, Donald and the boys boarded the plane for the ride that had cost Donald his car. "Listen, you chili-fed crook, this ride better be a large economy size, or I'll make you eat two dollars and ninety-eight cents' worth of your pezozies—without salt!" Donald

Boarding the Plane

threatened angrily.

The major took the controls and the plane rolled down the runway.

"Hang onto your seats, *señors!*" he said as the plane left the ground. "You are indeed een for a large ride."

"Wow! What a plane!" said Huey.

"Is he turning south, Unca Donald?" asked Dewey.

Donald was busy watching the town grow smaller and smaller as the plane climbed.

Airborne

"I don't know. I'm trying to see whose car is at Daisy's house," Donald answered. The next thing he knew, he was looking down on clouds. The town had disappeared, and the fields began to look like tiny squares on a checkerboard, but the plane continued to climb. The three boys, peering out of a round window, saw nothing but blue sky and clouds.

"Golly, we're high!" said Huey in a scared voice.

"I'm freezing," said Dewey as

A Spectacular View

he hugged himself and shivered.

"Is that Pablo trying to buzz the stars?" Louie asked.

All of a sudden the plane lurched.

"Buckle your safety belts, *señors!* I'm testing the controls," Pablo shouted. Donald and his nephews reached out, but they touched only the smooth sides of the plane.

"What safety belts?" Donald gasped as he fell.

Bonk! Bam! Bonk! Bam! The four of them were thrown around like rubber balls as the plane

Rough Ride

looped and rolled and plunged. Finally, one terrific jolt threw them all to the floor, knocking them unconscious.

Time flew. When Donald opened his eyes at last, he had no idea how long they had been in the air, nor how far they had traveled.

"Oooh! My head!" he groaned. "I must have been knocked out. Where are we?" He got up and looked out of the window. He shook his head. Was he imagining things?

"Great Willikens! We're flying

Coming To

through the biggest mountains I
ever saw!" Donald said. Then he
stifled a yell of fright. The plane
skimmed over a mountain crag so
close that it almost knocked an
eagle from its nest.

"Oooowoooo!" Donald groaned.
It took him a moment to catch his
breath after the hairbreadth escape. Then he shouted at Pablo,
"Hey! Look where you're going!"
He realized Pablo could not hear
him with the door to the control
cabin closed, so Donald opened it

Surprised Eagle

and frantically rushed in.

"Are you trying to kill us all?" Donald demanded.

Pablo was slumped down in the pilot's seat, his sombrero covering his face. Donald jerked it off, to find the Volcanovian quietly dozing with his feet propped against the stick.

"Of all the dumb things! This cluck is asleep!" Donald shrieked. He grabbed Pablo's arm and shook him. "Wake up! Wake up!" Donald's voice cracked with excitement

Asleep at the Controls

and fright, but Pablo's eyes stayed shut. Donald shook him again, and finally Pablo mumbled something. Donald bent closer to catch his words.

"Wake up, you say? What time ees eet, *señor?*" Pablo asked.

"It's forty-nine minutes after one. Wake up!" Donald pleaded.

Pablo yawned. "Eleven more minutes, *señor*. Een Volcanovia we always siesta until two," he said without opening his eyes.

Donald shuddered as he looked

"Wake Up!"

ahead and saw that they were flying into a narrow gorge.

"Wake up!" Donald yelled. He took another look at the sleeping Pablo, then hurried over to the co-pilot's seat and sat down.

"I can try to fly it myself," Donald said. He tried to move the stick, but it would not budge.

"He has the controls locked. I can't take over," Donald moaned. He tried again to awaken Pablo, but failed. Donald stared helplessly at the locked controls, then opened

Donald Tries the Controls

the door and went back to warn his frightened nephews.

Back in the pilot's cabin, Pablo was stirring at last. He yawned, stretched, and opened his eyes. He checked his watch.

"Must be about two o'clock," he said with another yawn.

He looked ahead, only to see the rocky wall of a mountain directly in front of the plane.

"Siesta ees over." Slowly he unlocked the controls and reached for the stick. A fraction of a second

"Siesta Ees Over."

later, the bomber's nose lifted.

Meanwhile, Donald, Huey, Louie, and Dewey, who huddled in the body of the plane, felt the sudden upward pull. Donald looked up.

"I guess that sleeping beauty came to. I'm going to give him a piece of my mind," Donald said. He stalked into the pilot room of the giant bomber.

"Take us home, you screwball. We've had enough!" Donald raged.

Pablo looked out of the side window and down, then shrugged. "But

Mountain Hopping

I can't, *señor*. I theenk I am lost!"
he confessed.

"Lost! He's *lost!* Oh, what a
drip," Donald shouted.

A deafening explosion took his
mind from his anger. As he looked
out, he saw giant rocks spurting
from the flaming and smoking
mountaintop.

"Volcanos! Get away from here!"
Donald screamed. He ran back to
reassure his nephews, who were
wide-eyed with fear. Pablo followed
him and held up his hands in a

Startling Sight

happy gesture as he smiled at Donald and his trembling nephews.

"Have no more fears, *señors*. I am no longer lost. We are *home*. We are een Volcanovia!" He beamed at them.

Donald looked out, but all he could see was a smoldering, smoking mass of volcanos. Pablo pointed to a tiny valley right in the midst of them. As they flew closer, little specks grew into groups of buildings that looked like a toy village in the foothills.

Volcanovia

"See eet? My home town—the capital of my contree," Pablo said proudly.

"The capital of Volcanovia, kids! No wonder we never saw it on a map!" Donald told his nephews.

"I never wanted to," said Huey.

"I don't want to now," said Louie.

"And I never want to see it again," said Dewey. The plane nosed downward, closer and closer to a tiny patch of smooth ground.

"Hey! You're not going to land,

An Impossible Landing

are you? We want to go home,"
Donald told Pablo.

"Sorry, *señors*. I must have forget," said Pablo.

"You can't stop this big plane
on this short field. You'll crash!"
Donald cried, but he could see that
his warning came too late. The
plane skimmed across the field and
rolled up the mountain at the end
of the runway. Donald was too
frightened to talk.

"Don' worry, *señor*. Eet weel
stop!" said Pablo. The plane

Short Runway

reached the peak of the mountain, then stopped with a jolting bump.

"See, *señor!*" Pablo said, his voice triumphant.

Donald looked out, scarcely able to believe that the perilous flight had ended. Then he went into action. He jerked open the door and leaped to the ground.

"I've had enough of that crazy pilot. I'm getting out of here while I'm still alive," he said.

WHOOM! Another volcano erupted. It was so close that Donald

A Lofty Perch

could feel the earth tremble. His hat flew high into the air. Donald, his knees shaking, retrieved his hat and scrambled back into the big bomber. His nephews looked as though they thought the world was coming to a hasty end, but Pablo was unconcerned.

"Take off! Fly anyplace. But get away from these volcanos!" Donald commanded. The boys looked outside where hot rocks were falling like hailstones. Pablo remained calm and cool. He looked at the

"Take Off!"

hailstones and laughed at Donald.

"Ha! Surely you not afraid of these leetle volcanos! They weel not hurt you," he said soothingly. Helping Donald to his feet, he pointed to a volcano that seemed to be the granddaddy of them all as it frowned down on them.

"But eef that beeg one over there, old Ferocio, ever blows hees top, then ees time to ron like the dee-kins," Pablo explained.

Donald and the boys looked at the huge mass of solid rock and

Old Ferocio

shuddered. Smaller volcanos were popping all around it.

"Just like the Fourth of July," said Huey.

Pablo moved to the door. He leaped out and, without bothering to look back to see whether the others followed, said, "Well, *señors*, eet ees time for lonch. Come weeth me. We'll go down to the ceety and have tamales and nice coconut milk." He waved his arm and set off down the hill without a backward glance.

Quick Exit

CHAPTER 3

STUCK IN VOLCANOVIA

Donald and his nephews stood stock still, watching Pablo's diminishing figure as he ran down the steep decline toward the capital of Volcanovia. Huey was the first to break the silence.

"We'd better follow," he said.

"There's no use staying here,"

Surefooted Pablo

Dewey pointed out.

"We can't take off," Louie added.

Donald nodded. He jumped out of the plane and caught the boys as they leaped out after him. They found that they were not as sure-footed as Pablo, and they skidded and slipped as they made their way down the mountainside.

"Maybe there's a train or bus that'll take us to the coast. We're going to leave this crazy place," Donald said with determination.

"Can't leave—" began Dewey.

Skidding Down the Mountain

"Too soon—" added Louie.

"To suit me," finished Huey.

A nearby blast sent them scurrying out of danger.

"Even the rock piles have volcanos in them!" Donald pointed out. He sat down on a small mound while he caught his breath.

FLOOP! A small hill near a fence blew up as they watched.

PUNG! The mound on which Donald sat exploded, sending Donald flying into the air. The boys gathered around it.

A Hot Seat

"A baby volcano!" said Huey.

"Isn't it—" said Louie.

"Cute?" asked Dewey.

PING! PING! PING! Three tiny piles of loose ground, hardly bigger than anthills, blew up under each of the little ducks, sending them up in the air. They hastily scrambled to their feet, not daring to sit anywhere. Donald jumped up and ran as fast as his legs would carry him toward the city.

"I can't get out of this country fast enough," he said.

PING! PING! PING!

The three boys picked up their heels and raced after him.

"That goes—" said Dewey.

"For us, too—" added Louie.

"Unca Donald," finished Huey.

They looked fearfully around at the popping volcanos as they hurried toward the town. Donald continued to run until he came to a railroad track. The four of them followed it to a railroad station, where an old relic of a train sat, parked on the tracks. A man was sitting with his back against the

Surrounded by Small Volcanos

station wall, sound asleep. Donald shook him, and the man awoke.

"When does this rusty train leave? We want to go to the coast," Donald said.

"Eet leave sometime, maybe, *señor*. But you can't take eet. You can't leave the contree—onless—" he drawled sleepily.

"Unless what?" Donald snapped.

"Onless you do something to make yourself a national hero. That ees our law," the man said.

Donald became angrier by the

"When Does This Train Leave?"

minute. He jumped up and down, shook one fist at the drowsy ticket agent, and frantically waved a handful of money with the other.

"You'd better sell me a ticket, or *else!*" Donald threatened.

The Volcanovian agent was unshaken by Donald's outburst. "You gat a medal from the President, an' I sell you a teekit," he repeated.

Donald turned away in disgust and went to hunt for Pablo. They found him at an outdoor lunch counter, busily eating a hot tamale.

Angry Donald

"Hey, Pablo. What's this business about being a national hero? What kind of a jam have you got me into?" Donald demanded. Pablo calmly continued his meal, swallowing some coffee before replying.

"You must do something of great benefeet to Volcanovia. That ees all, *señor*," he explained. He turned and continued eating, while Donald, disgusted and annoyed, awaited more of an explanation.

"What do you mean—benefit? Do I have to lick a couple of

Donald Demands an Explanation

armies?" Donald asked.

"Oh, no, *señor*," said Pablo.

He motioned toward a nearby building where half a dozen men crouched on their haunches, leaned against the wall.

"Just something easy, like invent soft sidewalks for the loafers to sit on," Pablo suggested.

Donald and the boys looked at each other. They were all thinking they had heard the silliest way of becoming a national hero that any one could think up, but Pablo had

Easy Living

still another suggestion to make.

"Or you might teach them how to live without working. They'd love that. Volcanovia ees the one contree een the world where only lazy people are welcomed to live," Pablo explained.

Donald was completely flabbergasted, but the boys tried to find some other way out.

"You left this Shangri-la to visit America," said Huey.

"What did you do to get permission—" began Louie.

Disgusted Ducks

"To leave?" asked Dewey.

Pablo leaned back comfortably and looked very proud.

"Me? Oh, I was a great discoverer!" he boasted.

Donald snorted. "Discoverer?" he said in a questioning tone.

"Yes, *señor*. I discovered that eef we siestaed two hours instead of one hour, we could skip a whole hour of work," Pablo said.

Donald was getting more and more disgusted, and the more disgusted he became, the more angry

Explaining His "Great Discovery"

he felt. He clenched his fists, and his shoulders shook with rage.

"To think that with all the swell countries around here, we get stuck in this one," he fumed. He shook his fists at Pablo.

"Why don't your lazy loafers do something to benefit themselves?" Donald demanded.

Pablo remained unruffled. "Oh, but, *señor*, they do. They rest all the time, which ees good for the body," said Pablo.

That made Donald completely

Donald Loses His Temper

lose his temper. "I'm going to d
something right now that will ben
fit the whole world," he cried. Wit
that, he made a flying leap towar
the grinning Volcanovian. "I'
going to punch your nose!"

The punch never landed. Pab
calmly raised one foot and kicke
Donald over backward. A secon
later, Donald was back on his fee
fists flying.

BOP! BAM! SOCK! The fighter
were hidden in the cloud of du
kicked up by their wild scuffle. Th

Leaping into Action

sleeping Volcanovians did not even make the effort to look up, but Donald's nephews were watching.

"Attaboy, Unca Donald! Hit him one for me," said Huey.

"And me, too!" said Louie.

"And me!" Dewey chimed in.

The dust subsided. Poor Donald was knocked flat on his face, out like a light. Pablo looked untouched.

"Already he learns to be a good Volcanovian. See? He takes a siesta," said Pablo.

Out Like a Light

CHAPTER 4

HOW NOT TO BE A HERO

Donald's three nephews stood guard. A few minutes passed, and Donald began to stir.

"I fell asleep. It must be the altitude," muttered Donald.

"You forgot—" said Huey.

"To duck—" said Dewey.

"A cloud," finished Louie.

Slow Recovery

Donald shook his head in an effort to clear it. A second later he remembered where he was and jumped to his feet. He walked determinedly down the street, motioning to his nephews to follow.

"Shake a leg, kids. We'll *walk* out of here," he said.

He found a policeman, leaning against a telegraph pole.

"Wake up, Sherlock! Which way do we go to reach the coast?" asked Donald.

Without opening his eyes, the

"Which Way to the Coast?"

policeman pointed toward a whole forest of erupting and smoking volcanos.

"That way, *señor*," he said.

One look in that direction convinced Donald and the boys that walking was out of the question.

"Well, it looks as though the only way to get out of here is to become a national hero," Donald said. His nephews nodded.

"Yes. Start thinking of something to do, Unca Donald," Huey said.

Obstacles

Donald sat on a rock and tried to think. Soon he suggested, "I can't think on an empty stomach. Let's grab a bite someplace."

Huey, Louie, and Dewey readily agreed and led the way to an open-air food stand.

"Four glasses of Grade A milk. And make it snappy," Donald told the man at the counter.

The man looked at Donald, then shook his head in a very sorrowful manner.

"We have nothing but coconut

"Four Glasses of Milk."

milk, *señor*," he said.

"I want real milk. Doesn't anybody ever milk these cows around here?" Donald asked, pointing to a pasture where cows were grazing.

"Nobody knows how, *señor*," the cook answered.

"Unca Donald, there's—" said Huey.

"Your—" added Louie.

"Chance!" finished Dewey.

"Chance?" asked Donald. He looked at them questioningly.

"You can teach the Volcanovian

Grazing Cows

people—" said Huey.

"To milk cows—" said Louie.

"And you'll become a national hero!" said Dewey.

Donald brightened. He jumped off the stool, ready to go into action at once.

"That's a deal. You kids get a crowd together, and I'll round up a cow," he said. He ran toward the cows, and the boys ran the other way. Donald dashed back to the counter and picked up a glass.

"In ten minutes we'll be on our

Sudden Activity

way home!" Donald said happily, stopping beside a cow. The cow lifted her head, but stood still.

"Don't even have to tie her. So, bossy," he said, patting the cow.

"Come one, come all! Free milking lesson by Professor Donald Duck!" he called in his loudest voice. A dignified old gentleman in a frock coat and a white beard and moustache came toward him. The man was astride a small, fat burro, and Huey hung on to the burro's tail.

Friendly Pat

"We couldn't get anybody to move, Unca Donald," Huey explained when they had come closer.

"So we brought the President!" Dewey announced.

"The President!" Donald gasped in surprise. Then he looked pleased. He would perform for the one person who could do him the most good in this very strange country of Volcanovia.

Never did I have such a break before, thought Donald as he began to milk the cow. "Watch this,

Milking the Cow

your honor," he said.

The President came closer, bent down, and peered over Donald's shoulder.

"See how simple it is, your lordship? Nothing to it," said Donald.

When the glass was filled to the brim with the fresh, warm milk, Donald stood up and faced the President of Volcanovia.

"There, your royal highness! Ambrosia fit for a king. Have a drink," he said, holding up the glass. The President was about to

"Have a Drink!"

accept the proffered glass with a
great show of dignity, when the
ceremony was interrupted. A loud
rumbling noise was heard, and, at
the same time, Donald began to
tremble. The President trembled;
Huey, Louie, and Dewey shook
from head to toe; and even the little
burro shook.

"What now?" Donald said out
loud. He looked at the ground and
found that the grass and trees were
also quivering. Even the rocks were
rattling. The glass in Donald's

A Shaky Interruption

hand shook violently.

"An earthquake!" Donald shouted. He knew there was nothing he could do but stand there until the rumbling and quaking stopped. Then he proceeded with the ceremony.

"Had me a little rattled there for a minute. But here, your majesty, have a drink," Donald said.

The Volcanovian President bowed slightly and reached for the glass. He held it up, ready to take a big swallow, while Donald waited,

On With the Ceremony

confident that his troubles were over. Then Donald gulped as he saw the President's face wrinkle up into a scowl.

"Dreenk thees?" asked the Volcanovian. He held the glass upside down, and a solid, yellow mass slid out into his hand. "How does one dreenk it—sliced?"

"Butter!" Donald exclaimed. He hastily grabbed the glass and ran toward the cow. "The earthquake churned the milk into butter! Wait! I'll get you another glass," he

Butter!

called back anxiously.

The cow kept right on eating grass, while Donald again put the glass under her. "So, bossy!" said Donald soothingly. Then he looked surprised. "Uh-oh!" he said.

His nephews looked at him questioningly. Donald groaned as he gave up the milking job.

"The earthquake also churned the cows. They're full of butter, too!" Donald complained.

The President of Volcanovia mounted his burro and rode away.

Another Try

Donald could think of no way to stop him. And Donald and his nephews, without a backward glance at the cows, walked back into town.

"You'd better get busy—" suggested Huey.

"And churn up another idea—" added Dewey.

"Unca Donald," finished Louie.

Donald turned furiously on them.

"Never mention the word 'churn' to me again," he warned.

Dejected Ducks

CHAPTER 5

JAILBIRDS

"What'll I do? What'll I do?" Donald asked himself as he paced up and down, back and forth, trying to think of a way to get out of Volcanovia. The Volcanovians had such queer ideas of what made a national hero. The three nephews, as worried as he, paced, too. Huey

What to Do?

was the first to stop.

"Pst! Unca Donald, there's a family row going on in this back-yard," he said, pointing over the wall.

Donald looked and saw a woman chopping wood, while a man with a tall silk hat squatted against the wall of the house and napped.

"It's the President's wife," Donald said. "Listen. She sounds angry."

"Every day I must spleet wood for the cook fire. I'm tired of eet

Hard at Work

too much," she complained. Her husband's answer was a snore.

Donald's interest was aroused when he noticed a tiny volcano erupting a few feet from where the woman was chopping the wood.

"Hmm. Maybe there's a chance here for me to do a great deed," he said aloud. He hopped over the wall and strutted over to the woman.

"Throw away your ax, madam! I'll show you how to save many hours of labor," Donald said.

Donald Offers to Help

She looked at him stupidly.

"Fetch your frying pan. I'll show you how to cook without firewood," Donald said. The President's wife went into the house and returned with her frying pan. "Now pour it full of squigwhistles, or whatever it is you wish to cook," Donald added.

She disappeared inside the house again, and, when she returned this time, the frying pan was filled with food.

Donald took the pan and held it

Filled Frying Pan

over the baby volcano. The pan got hot, and the food began to simmer.

"Nature put a stove in your backyard. Why not use it?" Donald asked her.

Instead of being impressed by Donald's good deed, the President's wife backed up, turned, and walked to the other end of the yard. She seemed to be frightened.

"But, *señor*, eet ees not safe!" she said as she retreated.

"Phooey!" Donald replied.

The flame from the volcano shot

Backyard Cookout

higher and higher, and Donald was pleased to see that the food was cooking so fast. He refused to worry about the natural stove, until he heard a rumbling sound coming from deep inside it.

"Don't get funny, squirt," Donald muttered.

The volcano rumbled all the more.

FOOP! The baby volcano blew up emitting rocks and steam and flame. The blast sent the frying pan and its steaming contents high

FOOP!

into the air. Donald and the President's wife ducked. The President of Volcanovia slept on.

PLOOP! The frying pan full of hot food made a wide arc and fell upside down on the head of the dignified President. It knocked off his top hat and spilled the gooey mass of food all over his head and face. He pulled the pan off, raving at poor, well-meaning Donald.

"Looks like Unca Donald missed the boat again," remarked Louie from behind the wall.

Rude Awakening

Donald stood and watched the President struggle. He felt helpless and worried, and he wondered what would come of the accident. Donald didn't need to see the man's face to know he was boiling with rage. His fists were clenched, and his voice shook as he turned toward Donald.

"So! Weeth treecks like thees you try to become a national hero," he growled. Donald was speechless, but the President had more to say.

"I, me, as Prasident of the most

Boiling With Rage

peaceful contree on earth, don' like
your meddling. From now on you
are branded een Volcanovia as a—"
he paused to point his forefinger in
Donald's face—"as *a National
Menace!*" His voice boomed and
was overheard by Volcanovians
who lived in the neighborhood.

One drowsing Volcanovian in a
nearby courtyard said to another,
"*A National Menace.*"

"The veesitor from America ees
a National Menace," repeated a
third man. And so the President's

"A National Menace!"

pronouncement spread to the marketplace.

"Deed you say *a National Menace?*" asked a dozing Volcanovian.

"Yes, I said *a National Menace,*" replied his friend, who was leaning against the building beside him.

The word continued to spread until it reached the judge of the high court of Volcanovia. Instead of taking his siesta crouched against a building, the judge slept in his swivel chair. Instead of the

Word Reaches the Judge

usual sombrero, his head was covered with a long white wig, the symbol of his high office. The news about Donald annoyed him.

"*A National Menace!* That means I must hold a trial!" he muttered.

He was not the only official irritated at the news. The jailer, in the usual sleeping pose of the snoozing Volcanovians, squatted against the jailhouse.

"*A National Menace* to be tried. That means I must work heem een

Sleepy Jailer

the salt mines. Phooey!" he mumbled under his breath.

Meanwhile Donald Duck, followed by his three nephews, was puzzled by the President's words, but he was completely unaware of the sensation the President's action had caused throughout Volcanovia.

"I wonder what happens to a guy who becomes a national menace," he said aloud. Huey, Louie, and Dewey shrugged. At that moment, a uniformed policeman grabbed Donald by the neck.

Under Arrest

"He ees arrested, *señor*," he said.

Donald, shackled with ball and chain, was soon brought before the high court of Volcanovia, where he found everyone asleep, except one individual with a briefcase, who sat at a table. One man reclined alone in the jury box. The bailiff leaned forward in his chair, his eyes closed. The guard slept in another chair.

Finally the judge opened one eye.

"Texas Tex, you're the only hombre een the jury box. Why

Courtroom Siesta

aren't the rest of the jurors here?" asked the judge.

The juror opened one eye.

"They said they couldn't sleep on these chairs. They're too hard," drawled Texas Tex.

"One juror ees enough. Get on weeth the trial while I take a siesta," the judge said, yawning and stretching.

"You can't try me in any such phony court. I demand my rights. I'm an American," Donald said, waving his fists.

"I Demand My Rights!"

The judge opened both eyes and sat up. He pointed a finger at Donald.

"An American, eh? You'll gat no favors from thees court onless you can prove eet," the judge said in a thundering voice.

Huey, Louie, and Dewey jumped to their feet and ran toward the exit.

"We'll get Pablo up here for you, Unca Donald," said Louie.

"He'll do it," said Dewey.

"Good old Pablo. He'll save my

An Accusing Finger

skin. He just has to!" Donald whispered to himself. He paced the floor while he waited to hear from the boys. All the other people in the courtroom dozed. Sometime later the boys returned, disappointment written all over their little faces.

"Unca Donald, Pablo won't be up to help you," reported Louie.

"He's taking a siesta, and we couldn't wake him," explained Huey.

A voice from the jury box interrupted them. Texas Tex was

Pacing the Floor

awake and ready to talk.

"Stop makin' so much jaw music. How can the jury sleep?" he said.

Donald gave him a withering look and turned back to the boys.

"Unca Donald, have you got a lawyer?" asked Dewey.

"I—I suppose so," Donald said in a doubtful voice.

"Maybe that's him. Ask," said Louie, pointing to the person at the council table. Donald went over to him.

"You're the only guy that's

A Sign of Hope

awake around here. Maybe you're my lawyer, huh?" Donald asked.

The lawyer stopped taking papers from his briefcase long enough to glare at Donald. Then he pointed to a chair at the other end of the room, where another Volcanovian was soundly sleeping.

"I'm the state's lawyer. That's your lawyer over there," the counselor said.

Donald stared and felt more hopeless. The lawyer for the Volcanovian state got up and walked

Donald's Lawyer

to the jury box. He shook Texas Tex by the elbow in an attempt to awaken him.

"Wake up, jury. To make thees trial legal you have to grunt louder than you snore," he said.

The juryman looked up.

"The prisoner claims to be an American. Are you not an American, too, Texas Tex?" the attorney asked.

"Yup. Afore I was run out of San Antone," Tex drawled.

The lawyer leaned so far forward

Waking the Jury

that his nose was in the juryman's face. Tex drew back.

"As a former American, do you see any wrong een finding thees other American guilty?" the lawyer demanded.

"Just a minute afore I answer that," said Texas Tex. He lazily turned in his chair until he faced Donald.

"Is you-all from Texas, podner?" he asked.

"No," Donald whispered back.

Tex turned back to the lawyer

"Is You-All From Texas, Podner?"

and shrugged. "He ain't from Texas, suh. So I'd say the varmint could be guilty of anything."

The state's lawyer wore a smug and self-satisfied expression as he went over to rouse the judge.

"Wake up, your honor. The jury has found the prisoner guilty. Pronounce sentence so I can take a siesta, too!" he shouted.

Donald and the boys could hardly believe such a thing could happen, even in Volcanovia, but the judge merely nodded and waved his hand.

Guilty!

A guard came to get Donald.

The trial over, Donald was locked in jail, with a guard stationed outside his cell. Finally the warden walked past and Donald heard him grumbling to himself.

"I must make heem work. Phooey! Plenty of time *mañana*," he was saying. There was nothing Donald could do about it, but at least he had one day of grace.

Meanwhile Huey, Louie, and Dewey hid behind some bushes, trying to figure out some way of saving

Sad Prisoner

their Uncle Donald.

"If the guard goes to sleep, we'll sneak up and let Unca Donald out," suggested Louie.

"Good idea. Everybody sleeps in Volcanovia," said Huey.

"We'll just wait until we catch him at it," said Dewey. They waited in the bushes. At last the guard began to yawn and stretch his arms, casually letting his gun rest across his lap.

"Aha! He's getting sleepy now," whispered Dewey. They stayed in

Keeping Watch

their hiding place until they saw the guard's chin sink to his chest and they could hear his steady snoring. Then they slowly crept from their hiding place behind the bushes.

"Now's—" said Louie.

"Our—" said Huey.

"Chance," finished Dewey.

But the little plotters had reckoned without the queer forces of nature in Volcanovia. A volcano close at hand chose that moment to erupt. PONK! A rock hit Dewey,

Cautious Approach

and he was knocked out. BONG!
Another rock struck Huey on the
head. THUMP! A third rock put
Louie to sleep. The three were
stretched out in front of Donald's
door.

Inside the cell, the sound of the
guard's snoring aroused Donald.
He looked out through the bars and
smiled with pleasure.

"The guard is taking a siesta.
Now if the kids would sneak up
and take his keys—" Donald said.
Then he saw the boys. "The kids

PONK! BONG! THUMP!

are taking a siesta, too!" he
groaned. He felt that the boys had
let him down when he needed them
the most.

Poor Donald spent a miserable
night.

"Nobody loves me anymore," he
sobbed into the darkness, wondering whether he would ever know
freedom again.

Unhappy Donald

CHAPTER 6

MOTHER NATURE STEPS IN

At dawn, Donald's three little nephews lifted their dizzy heads from the hard ground and looked around them.

"Something must have knocked us out," said Louie.

"We've been asleep for hours," said Dewey.

Morning

"I still feel groggy," said Huey.

"Anything could have happened to Unca Donald in that time," said Louie, looking worried.

"Unca Donald—" began Huey in a small voice.

"Are—are you—" added Louie in a frightened stammer.

"Still there?" gulped Dewey.

They listened fearfully for a reply.

"Yes! You little ingrates! You bums! You loafers!" thundered Donald from inside the jail cell.

"You Loafers!"

"He's still alive," said Huey.

"Very much so," said Louie. Dewey just giggled with relief. The three boys looked around, wondering what to do next to help Donald.

"We can't get to the jail door now," said Dewey.

"The guard's awake," Louie agreed.

They heard someone coming toward the cell.

"That isn't the worst possible news. Look who else is awake," said Huey, looking over his shoulder.

Change of Plans

The jailer was walking toward Donald's cell, carrying a rope and muttering to himself.

"May as well get the job over weeth. He won't last long een the mines. Poor faller," he said. That was too much for Huey and Louie and Dewey to stand. Louie gave the signal, and they went into action.

"You can't take our uncle," squealed Louie.

"You slave driver!" shouted Dewey.

The three of them tackled the

The Jailer Approaches

big Volcanovian, Huey grabbing his left leg, Dewey his right, and Louie tackling his waist with a flying leap. As the jailer fell to the ground, he whipped the serape from around his neck, scooped the boys onto it, and lifted it up by the corners to form a big bag.

"Geeves trouble from these shrimps. I feex," said the jailer. He gave the squirming bundle an angry shake as he opened the door of another cell and dumped the bag inside.

Flying Tackle

"Thees empty cell weel hold you for a while!" he growled.

Plop, plop, plop, the boys tumbled to the floor. They picked themselves up quickly, but they were too late. The jail door had clanged shut, and the jailer turned the key.

"You can't do this to us!" shrieked Louie.

"We're junior members of the Bear Cub Rangers!" yelled Huey.

"We'll report you to the Chief Grizzly!" threatened Dewey. But no one paid any attention to them

Thrown into Jail

except Donald, who sat dejectedly on the floor of his cell as he wept bitterly.

"I'm doomed. The kids are locked up, and the jailer is rattling at my door," he wailed. The boys heard him and began to cry, too.

"Good-bye, Unca Donald," sobbed Louie.

"Good-bye, boys. Be good to your grandma," Donald said sorrowfully.

For a while there was nothing but gloomy silence. Then Donald

"Good-Bye, Unca Donald."

heard the guard and the jailer talking. They were walking toward the door to Donald's jail cell.

RUMBLE! Another sound broke the jail's stillness. It echoed not only in the building but all around.

"Uh-oh! Where have I heard that rumble before?" Donald asked himself. He began to quiver and tremble.

"Ron for your life! Eet ees wan beeg earthquake!" shouted the guard. He whirled around and ran just as fast as he could away from

Earthquake!

the jailhouse. The jailer was right at his heels.

Donald Duck, meanwhile, was frightened half to death. He shook from head to foot, and the whole room shook with him. Then the walls and ceiling began to crack, and plaster fell in big chunks all around him, forming large piles of debris.

"The whole jail is caving in on me," he said. The boys, in the next cell, were just as scared.

"Good-bye again," called Huey.

Frightened Half to Death

"S'long," said Louie.

"This time for sure," said Dewey.

CRACK! CRASH! There was a tremendous sound of cracking and splintering, and, the next thing Donald and the boys knew, they were in the great out-of-doors!

"The walls fell over," Donald said in surprise.

"Yeah! Earthquakes do funny things," said Dewey, brushing himself off. All four of them looked at each other and grinned. Louie was

Free at Last

the first to come to his senses.

"Well, what are we standing here for? We're free!" he said.

That was a signal to the others. They picked up their heels and ran like greased lightning. They zipped past the guard and jailer, who had stopped running when the earth ceased its trembling.

"Deed you see four streaks pass just now, going toward the hills?" asked the jailer.

"Yes, I think eet was our prisoners," said the guard. The pair

Fast Escape

just looked at each other and
shrugged helplessly.

"Weeth the prisoners gone, I haf
no job. And weeth the jail gone, you
haf no job," said the jailer, "so—"

"So we're free," said the guard
happily. The jailer smiled, too, and
they began to figure out what to do
with their unexpected freedom.
Being Volcanovians, they had but
one thought in mind. They hurried
to the nearest tree and slumped
down against it.

"Let's celebrate," said the jailer.

Out of Their Jobs

"Yes. Weeth wan beeg siesta!" murmured the guard drowsily. So, while their prisoners continued their sprint toward the hills, the Volcanovians peacefully snoozed.

When Donald and his nephews reached a safe spot a long way from town, they sat down to get their breath and rest.

"What a spot we're in. No way to get out of this place, and no hope for us if we stay," Donald said.

"Oh, if there were only some way for me to become a national hero,"

A Quiet Celebration

he added with a sigh.

Huey, Louie, and Dewey sat up, listening.

"Unca Donald, we keep hearing a rumbling sound!" said Dewey.

"But there's no earthquake," Louie pointed out. They looked fearfully around and saw the biggest volcano of them all quaking in the background. Louie pointed to it.

"Look! It's old Ferocio getting ready to explode!" he yelled.

That was all the four needed to

About to Explode

make them forget how tired they were. They leaped to their feet and began running again, this time toward town.

"Pablo said that if Ferocio ever blows, the people will have to run like the dickens," Donald said. Soon they were running down the streets of the capital city of Volcanovia.

"Unca Donald, the people don't know their danger. They are sleeping. It's siesta time," Dewey said. Donald kept right on running. Dewey got ahead of him and

Fleeing From Old Ferocio

stopped suddenly, gesturing wildly.

"Wait! If we wake them, we'll save their lives, and—" said Dewey. Donald understood then what he meant.

"I get it. We'll be national heroes!" he cried excitedly. He told the boys to scatter and awaken everyone they came across. He rushed over to a group sleeping against the wall, but he soon realized that the job was almost hopeless. The boys came back a few minutes later, tired and exhausted.

A Hopeless Task

"They won't wake up," Donald said.

"I tried sticking them with pins," said Dewey wearily.

"I threw water on them, but they still sleep," Huey said.

"The mountain's rumbling louder. There won't be time to get the people out of town anyhow," Louie said.

"Only thing to do is stop the eruption!" Donald said.

"But how?" asked Louie.

"Find Pablo. We must fly over

Discussing Strategy

the volcano and drop something in its throat to plug it up," Donald said.

They ran around looking for Pablo. Donald found him huddled against a wall, peacefully sleeping, of course.

"There he is! Now if I can wake him!" Donald said. He grabbed Pablo by the hair and shook him as hard as he could. "Wake up, Pablo. It's up to us to save your country!"

Pablo snored. Donald shook him again. Dewey ran up to him holding

"Wake Up, Pablo!"

a handful of red things.

"Ram a handful of these hot peppers down his throat, Unca Donald," Dewey said.

Donald grabbed the peppers and jerked open Pablo's mouth. GUG! BLUB! Strange noises came from Pablo as Donald stuffed the peppers into him. But they made him wake up. He jumped two feet into the air, clutching his throat.

"Fire! Breemstone! What geefs! I'm borning op!" shrieked Pablo. He jumped up and down like a

"I'm Borning Op!"

grasshopper, then started to run. He ran toward a swimming pool and jumped into the water, fully dressed.

"Pablo, look! Old Ferocio is going to blow up," Donald said, running toward the edge of the pool.

Pablo popped his head up out of the water, and his hair stood on end in fright. "Old Ferocio!" he shouted. He fell all over himself in his haste to scramble out of the pool. "Oh, my goodness, *señor*. We are doomed," he moaned.

"We Are Doomed!"

"There's still time to plug it up," Donald said.

"Weeth what?" asked Pablo.

"I hadn't thought of that," said Donald.

His nephews had been working on the answer to that problem. They had found a huge pile of baskets stacked next to a warehouse a few yards away.

"There are tons of stuff in those baskets," said Louie.

"If we could drop them into the volcano—" said Dewey.

The Boys Have an Idea

"I'll taxi the plane down here. We'll load eet and take off. Eet ees the only hope for Volcanovia," Pablo said.

He ran at top speed toward the hill where the giant bomber had been landed and lost no time maneuvering it into position beside the warehouse. Then he hurried to help Donald and the boys load the heavy baskets on the plane. For the first time in his life, Pablo really worked!

The plane was quickly loaded,

Loading the Plane

and soon they were flying toward
old Ferocio. As the bomber approached the crater, they could see
that the volcano was already begin-
ning to blaze.

"I am ready to buzz the crater,
señor. Stand by to drop the load,"
Pablo called. He nosed the plane
up, checked their position, and
ordered, "Bombs away!"

FOOF! HIC! The volcano sput-
tered as the huge load of heavy
baskets descended into the crater
opening.

Direct Hit

"Bull's-eye! Old Ferocio ees plugged up tight," cried Pablo, looking back.

"*Volcanovia is saved!*" yelled Donald and his nephews.

"I'll be a national hero now. Not a shadow of a doubt," Donald said.

"Unca Donald did it!" said Huey.

"We can go home!" said Dewey.

"Yippee!" said Louie.

But their merriment ceased suddenly when Dewey asked, "Say, did anybody look to see what was in those baskets?"

"Volcanovia Is Saved!"

"I didn't," said Louie.

"I didn't," said Huey.

"I hope it was cement. Pab, fly back over the crater to see if everything is all right," Donald suggested. Pablo circled back, while Donald looked through a window. His eyes opened wide.

"The mountain is acting funny," he reported. "There's white stuff oozing out of the top."

The white mass shot higher and higher and higher into the air. The boys drew around Donald, trying

Strange Results

to guess what it was. Some of it flew right up next to the plane.

"Popcorn!" cried Donald.

"Fly for your life! We'll be snowed under!" Donald called to Pablo. As they flew over Volcanovia, they could see the whole capital city was covered with drifts.

"The whole country is being buried in popcorn," Donald moaned.

"One minute I'm a national hero, the next I'm a national menace. I'll never get out of Volcanovia," Donald said in despair.

Snowing Popcorn

Huey, Louie, and Dewey wore mournful expressions. Pablo was the only one who seemed undisturbed by the fate they had in store for them. He smiled peacefully.

"Oh, yes, you weel. We're all leaving," he said.

"All?" asked Donald.

"After thees day's work I'll never dare show my face een Volcanovia, either," said Pablo.

Donald and the boys were happy to look down for their last view of Volcanovia.

Heading Home

After a long and uneventful flight, Pablo finally landed the bomber on home soil. All five of the occupants lost no time in leaping out of the plane.

"Good old U.S.A.," said Donald.

"Come, *señor*, we must sign the ragister at the airport," said Pablo.

"Wait a minute!" said Huey.

"What became—" said Dewey.

"Of Unca Donald?" finished Louie.

Pablo stopped and looked back.

"Do you suppose—" said Huey.

Donald Is Missing

"He climbed back—" said Louie.

"In the plane?" finished Dewey.

There was nothing for them to do but to go back and investigate. Then they noticed something resting against the big landing wheel. Closer inspection showed the something to be Donald Duck, peacefully reclining in true Volcanovian fashion, with his eyes closed.

"Look at that!" Huey said.

"He's taking—" said Dewey.

"A siesta!" finished Louie.

"Z-Z-Z," said Donald.

Siesta Time!

Other **BIG LITTLE BOOKS**® Available

* With "FLIP-IT" cartoons

LASSIE—The Shabby Sheik

THE LONE RANGER Outwits Crazy Cougar

MICKEY MOUSE—Adventure in Outer Space

MICKEY MOUSE—Mystery at Disneyland

* **THE PINK PANTHER—**Adventure in Z-Land

POPEYE—Danger, Ahoy!

POPEYE—Ghost Ship to Treasure Island

* **POPEYE—**Queen Olive Oyl

* **ROAD RUNNER—**The Super Beep-Catcher

TOM AND JERRY Meet Mr. Fingers

TWEETY AND SYLVESTER—The Magic Voice

WOODY WOODPECKER—The Meteor Menace

* With "FLIP-IT" cartoons

GOLDEN® Full-Length Adventures

75163-6379